For our wonderful sons,
Daniyal, Adam and Haris.

Razzaq Publishing UK
Email: RazzaqPublishing@gmail.com
First Published in Great Britain 2021 by Razzaq Publishing.
Copyright Arfan Razzaq

Mr Smarty-Pants got his name because he uses his pants in a very smart way to solve problems.

One day, at the airport, the handle of Mr Smarty-Pants' suitcase broke.

2

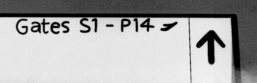
He had a smart idea! "I will use my pants to make a handle," announced Mr Smarty-Pants.

People nearby giggled and agreed, "that must be Mr Smarty-Pants!"

Mr Smarty-Pants went on a parachuting trip. On the aeroplane he realised that he had forgotten his parachute.

He had a smart idea! "I will use my pants as a parachute," gasped Mr Smarty-Pants.

People nearby giggled and agreed, "that must be Mr Smarty-Pants!"

Mr Smarty-Pants and his friends were writing messages and putting them into a bottle for sailors to find. However, Mr Smarty-Pants did not have any paper.

He had a smart idea! "I will use
my pants to write a message,"
declared Mr Smarty-Pants.

People nearby giggled and agreed,
"that must be Mr Smarty-Pants!"

Spring had arrived, Mr Smarty-Pants visited an adventure park only to find that the zip-wire seat was broken.

He had a smart idea! "I will use my pants to slide down the zip wire," insisted Mr Smarty-Pants.

People nearby giggled and agreed, "that must be Mr Smarty-Pants!"

Mr Smarty-Pants loved playing
Robin Hood with his bow and arrow.
The string of his bow broke.

He had a smart idea! "I will use
my pants in place of a string,"
uttered Mr Smarty-Pants.

People nearby giggled and agreed,
"that must be Mr Smarty-Pants!"

11

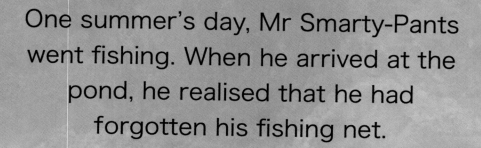

One summer's day, Mr Smarty-Pants
went fishing. When he arrived at the
pond, he realised that he had
forgotten his fishing net.

He had a smart idea! "I will use a stick and knot up my pants to make a fishing net," muttered Mr Smarty-Pants.

People nearby giggled and agreed, "that must be Mr Smarty-Pants!"

13

On his visit to the High Street shops, Mr Smarty-Pants saw two robbers in a bank.

He had a smart idea! "I will put my pants over my trousers, like a super-hero, and scare the robbers away," whispered Mr Smarty-Pants.

People nearby giggled and agreed, "that must be Mr Smarty-Pants."

On an autumn's evening, Mr Smarty-Pants was walking home from work. He slipped on the leaves and hurt his arm.

He had a smart idea! "I will use my pants to make a sling for my arm," cried Mr Smarty-Pants.

People giggled and agreed, "that must be Mr Smarty-Pants!"

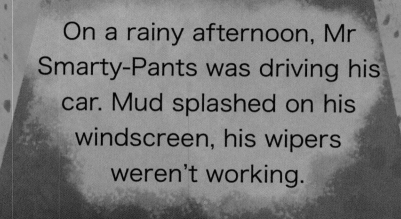

On a rainy afternoon, Mr
Smarty-Pants was driving his
car. Mud splashed on his
windscreen, his wipers
weren't working.

SM45 PAN

He had a smart idea! "I will use my pants to clean the windscreen," suggested Mr Smarty-Pants.

People nearby giggled and agreed, "that must be Mr Smarty-Pants!"

19

On a winter's day, Mr Smarty-Pants
saw a broken down car and tow-truck.
However, the tow-truck had no rope to
pull the car to the garage for repair.

He had a smart idea! "I will use
my pants instead of a rope,"
boasted Mr Smarty-Pants.

People nearby giggled and agreed,
"that must be Mr Smarty-Pants!"

Can you be like Mr Smarty-Pants?
What smart ways can you think of to
use and recycle clothes?

Mr Smarty-Pants used his pants in a clever way to solve problems.

ISBN 978-1-8384394-0-8

THIS BOOK BELONGS TO

....

Lila was very nervous when she felt her front tooth wiggle for the first time.

She had heard from her sister
that when you lose a tooth, it
hurts a lot and you bleed a lot.
She didn't want to lose her tooth.
She liked her smile the way it was.

She tried to ignore her tooth and hoped it would stop wiggling. She ate soft foods, drank through a straw, and brushed her teeth gently. She avoided biting anything hard or sticky.

She asked her mom to help her keep her tooth in, but she said it was better to let it fall out naturally.

One day, she was having lunch at
school with her friends. She was
eating a cheese sandwich when she
felt something hard in her mouth.
She spit it out and saw her tooth
on her napkin. She felt a slight pain
in her gum and tasted blood. She
panicked and started to cry.

She ran to the nurse's office and showed her her tooth. The nurse gave her a tissue and a small plastic bag to keep her tooth safe.

She told her not to worry and that losing a tooth was a normal part of growing up. She also told her about the tooth fairy and how she would come and leave her a surprise under her pillow if she put her tooth there.

Lila had never heard of the tooth fairy before. She wondered what kind of surprise she would get. She hoped it would be something nice and not scary.

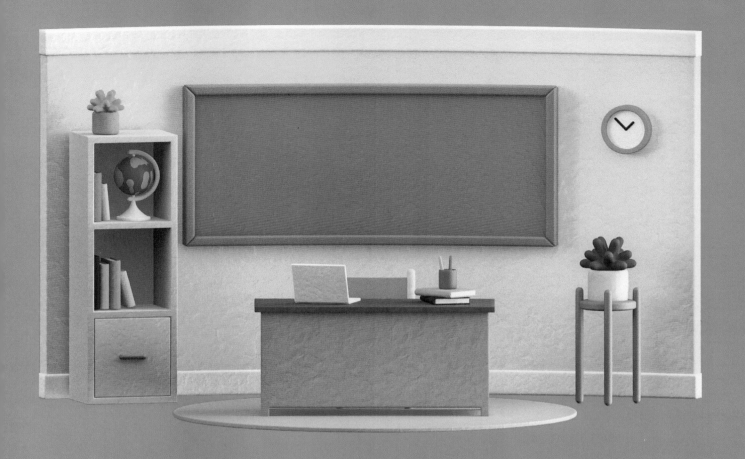

She calmed down and went back to class. She showed her teacher and classmates her tooth. They congratulated her and said she was lucky to get a visit from the tooth fairy.

She couldn't wait to get home and show her mom and dad and sister her tooth. She put it in her backpack and ran to the bus. She sat next to her best friend Mia and told her what happened. Mia hugged her and said she had lost four teeth already and got a dollar each time from the tooth fairy.

Lila wondered how much she would get for her tooth. She hoped it would be enough to buy a new doll. She had been saving up for one for a long time.

When she got home, she showed her mom and dad and sister her tooth. They were happy for her and said she was growing up fast. They told her to rinse her mouth with water and brush her teeth gently. They also told her to put her tooth under her pillow before she went to bed.

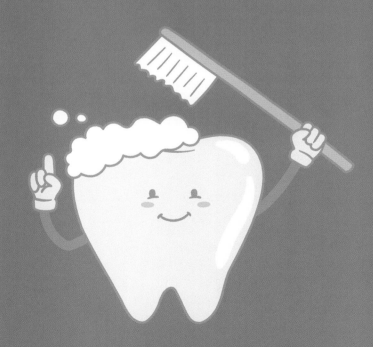

Lila did as they said and went to bed early that night. She put her tooth under her pillow and closed her eyes. She dreamed of the tooth fairy coming to visit her and leaving her a surprise.

She woke up the next morning and reached under her pillow. She felt something cold and hard. She pulled it out and saw a shiny coin. It was a quarter.

Lila was disappointed. She had expected something more exciting than a quarter. She had hoped for a dollar or a toy or a candy.

She got out of bed and ran to her parents' room. She showed them the quarter and asked them if that was all the tooth fairy gave.
They smiled and hugged her. "It's ok" they said.

That night, in her bed, she was angry and disappointed. She put her quarter under her pillow, closed his eyes and tried to sleep.
She dreamed of the tooth fairy. She was a real fairy with wings and a wand. She had a big bag full of surprises. She flew into his room and took his quarter from under his pillow.
She smiled and said:
"Thank you for your quarter, Lila. It's just what I needed for my collection."
She threw his quarter into her bag and flew away.

Lila woke up with a start. She was sweating and shaking. She realized it was just a dream. But it felt so real.

She looked under his pillow. Her quarter was gone.

She felt a surge of panic. She searched his bed, his floor, his drawers, but she couldn't find it anywhere.
She saw a small envelope on their nightstand. She opened it and saw a note and a dollar bill inside.
The note said:

Dear Lila,

I'm sorry if I confused you with my last visit. I was just having some fun with you. But I realized that you were not happy with their prank or mine. So I decided to give you your tooth back and apologize for my mischief. I hope you forgive me and for my joke. I love you very much and I'm proud of you for losing your first tooth.

I also decided to give you a gift to make up for my mistake. It's a necklace with a pendant that looks like your tooth. It's made of silver and has your name engraved on it. It's very beautiful and unique, just like you.

You can wear it around your neck and always remember this special moment in your life. You can also show it to your friends and family and tell them about your adventures with the tooth fairy.

I hope you like this surprise better than the dollar or the quarter. It's from the real tooth fairy. The one who cares about you and your smile.

I hope you enjoy your new smile and your new necklace.

Love,

The Tooth Fairy"

u

Lila couldn't believe it. The real tooth fairy had come back and given her her tooth back.
She had also given her a necklace with a pendant that looked like her tooth.
It was the most beautiful thing she had ever seen.

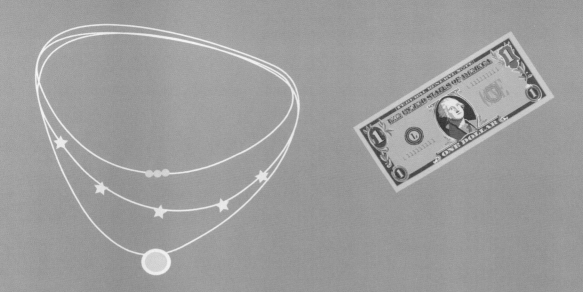

She put the necklace around her neck
and looked at herself in the mirror.
She smiled and saw her gap where
her tooth used to be.
She didn't mind it anymore.
She liked her new smile.
She liked her new necklace.
She liked the real tooth fairy and
forgived her.

She ran to her parents'
room and opened the
door.
"Mom! Dad! Look what
the real tooth fairy
gave me!" she said.
Her parents woke up
and saw her smiling
face and sparkling
necklace.
They smiled and hugged
her.
"Lila, we're so happy
for you," they said.

They also told her they loved her very much and that they were proud of her for losing her first tooth.

She told them she loved them too and that she was proud of herself for losing her first tooth.

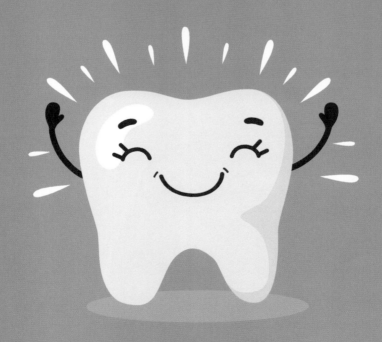

She also told them about her dreams and how the real tooth fairy had visited.

They listened to her story with interest and amusement.

They laughed and cried together.

They celebrated Lila's milestone
with joy and gratitude.
They thanked the real tooth
fairy for making Lila happy and
giving her a gift that she would
cherish forever.

Printed in Great Britain
by Amazon